MW00934425

Benny Bee

Copyright © 2020 Delsa K. Dislers
All rights reserved
First Edition

Fulton Books, Inc.
Meadville, PA

Published by Fulton Books 2020

ISBN 978-1-64952-005-0 (paperback)
ISBN 978-1-64952-006-7 (digital)

Printed in the United States of America

Benny Bee

Delsa K. Dislers

It was a nice sunny day. Benny the honeybee could hear some of the neighborhood kids playing outside. Oh, how Benny wanted to find a friend. Every time Benny would fly near someone, they would scream and run away. This made Benny sad. He didn't understand why no one wanted to be his friend.

3

Benny noticed a little girl playing in her front yard. She looked very nice. Benny flew over near her. She did what most people do when he flew near; she screamed and ran away.

Benny followed her, yelling as loud as he possibly could, "Please, I just want to be your friend."

The little girl heard Benny and stopped running.

Benny said sweetly, "Won't you be my friend?"

"Well, if you promise not to sting me, I will be your friend."

Benny agreed that he would not sting her. He explained that honeybees don't enjoy stinging people. They only sting people if they feel scared or threatened. The little girl was very happy to hear this. Benny asked the little girl her name.

"I'm Kiki," she said.

"I'm Benny," he said.

"So very nice to meet you," they both said at the very same time.

They laughed and laughed, and their friendship began.

Benny and Kiki became best friends. They were together almost all the time. They tried to teach people that they did not need to be afraid of bees; they just need to be careful not to scare them.

Benny had to convince his bee friends and family that most people are actually pretty nice; they just don't want to get stung.

Kiki and Benny loved playing at the park and smelling the pretty flowers. Benny would fly up onto Kiki's ear so that she could hear him. Sometimes when Kiki was talking to Benny, people thought that she was talking to herself.

She did not care what other people thought; she was just so happy to have her new best friend. She loved Benny, and Benny loved Kiki.

Bee Kind

About the Author

Delsa, a gymnast at age five, is now a coach whose passion is bringing joy to children. She loves laughing, dancing at parties, making up stories with her granddaughter Kiki, and making art from sea glass.

CPSIA information can be obtained
at www.ICGtesting.com
Printed in the USA
BVHW020732240221
600911BV00012B/886

9 781649 520050